MY CHRISTMAS TREASURY

A Collection of Christmas Stories, Poems, and Songs

PICTURES BY LOWELL HESS

MERRIGOLD PRESS

NEW YORK

CHRISTMAS IS COMING

Christmas is coming,
  the geese are getting fat;
Please to put a penny
  in the old man's hat;

If you haven't a penny,
  a ha'penny will do;
If you haven't got a ha'penny,
  God bless you.

A CHRISTMAS FOR BEARS

BY RAY ST. CLAIR

THERE WAS a bear who did not believe in Santa Claus, or in Christmas either. Each year, at the first sign of cold weather, he would curl up in his cave and sleep until spring. Naturally, he did not believe in Christmas.

This year, however, he could not get to sleep. He tossed and turned, and at last, he staggered to his feet.

Since he could not sleep, he would go out and see for himself that there was no Santa Claus and no Christmas. So he came out of his cave and sniffed the cold wind.

"What a climate!" he grumbled.

While he was trying to decide which way he should go, he heard a loud whirring overhead. "Helicopter?" he asked himself. "Four-motor transport? Mail plane?"

Suddenly there was a loud thump, off in the woods.

"Wreck!" shouted the bear. "I must help them!" And off he lumbered.

It was not a helicopter, nor a four-motor transport, nor even a mail plane. When the bear reached the spot, puffing because he had run so hard, he saw only an old-fashioned sleigh on its side, with bundles scattered in the snow all around it. A stout gentleman with white whiskers was yelling and jumping up and down in the snow.

"My," thought the bear, "he

certainly does seem upset. I wonder who he is."

"Vixen!" shouted the stout gentleman. "Blitzen!"

Then the stout gentleman saw the bear. "So!" he said accusingly. "A bear, right out in the open at Christmas time. No wonder my reindeer got scared and ran away!"

"I'm sorry," the bear apologized. "I didn't mean any harm. I just couldn't get to sleep."

The stout gentleman patted the bear's head. "Don't feel bad," he said in a kindly tone. "We all have our off days. Only, I wish it hadn't happened right in the middle of the rush season."

"But I do feel bad about it," insisted the bear. "Isn't there anything I can do?"

The stout gentleman gazed thoughtfully at the bear. "Maybe," he said, tapping his nose. "Would you *really* help me?"

"Of course!" said the bear.

First they got the sleigh back on its runners. Then they loaded all the bundles onto it.

"Now what?" asked the bear. "Shall I chase your reindeer back?"

"No!" said the stout gentleman hastily. "They will find their way home. I want you to take their place and help with deliveries."

The bear was shocked. "No!" he shouted. "I'm no horse."

The stout gentleman sighed. "Lots of good children," he said, "are going to be disappointed."

"Oh, all right!" said the bear crossly. "Hitch me up."

"You're a good bear!" said the stout gentleman, fastening the lines around the bear's shoulder. Then, "Giddyap!" he called, and they were off.

"Hey!" shouted the bear over his shoulder. "I'm flying!"

"Of course you are," replied the stout gentleman. "We have a lot of calls to make, and you can't cover the territory by staying on the ground."

They made call after call, landing each time on the roof of the house. At every house the stout gentleman would swing a huge

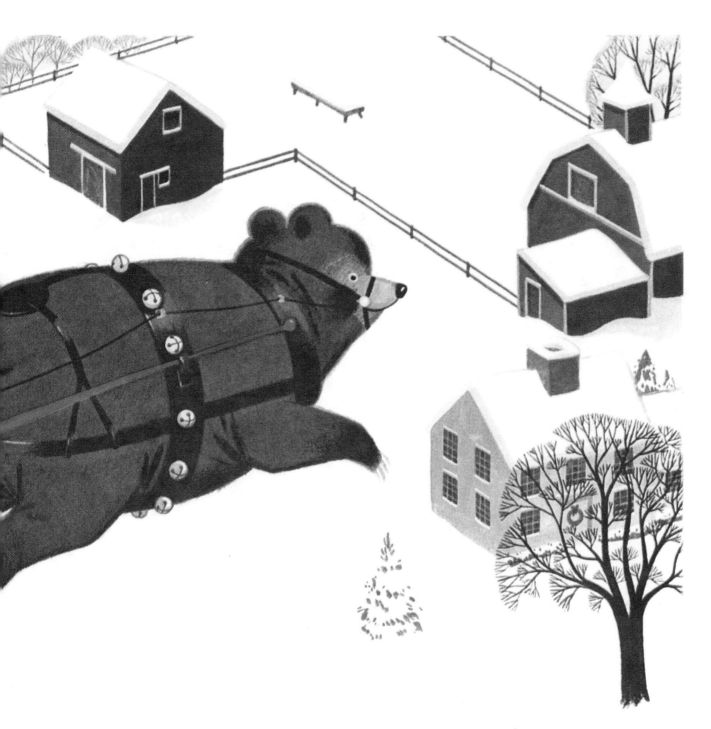

pack onto his back from the sleigh; then, quick as a flash, he would slide down the chimney.

At last, as the sky began to lighten in the east, they made their last call. The bear sighed gratefully. Now, he was tired enough to sleep the rest of the winter.

The stout gentleman stuck his head up out of this last chimney and beckoned to the bear.

"Come with me," he said. "I want to show you something."

"I'm too fat to get down that chimney," objected the bear. But before he knew it he *was* down, standing beside the stout gentleman in a small bedroom.

In one corner of the room were two children sound asleep in bed. In another was a pine tree festooned with popcorn and bright colored balls. Underneath were toys: skates, and dolls, and books.

"These children would not have had a Christmas tree or any gifts if it hadn't been for you," said the stout gentleman. "You're a good bear, a noble and unselfish bear."

The bear wriggled and sighed. He didn't understand this talk about Christmas trees any more than the talk about Santa Claus.

When the gentleman said good-by, the bear was so tired he could hardly crawl back into his cave. Before you could say "Merry Christmas," he was sound asleep.

And then suddenly he woke up, with the warm spring sun pouring in on him. It was time to get up.

"What a curious dream!" he muttered, staggering to his feet.

Then he turned his head and saw it. It wasn't a dream at all. It was a Christmas tree for bears.

There was a note on white paper that read:

To my best friend, the bear, who helped me bring a merry Christmas to all the children. With most heartfelt best wishes,

SANTA CLAUS

"Santa Claus!" exclaimed the bear. "So there really is a Santa Claus, and a Christmas—" he dipped his paw into the comb of honey—"for bears."

O COME, ALL YE FAITHFUL

O come, all ye faithful, joyful and triumphant,
O come ye, O come ye to Bethlehem;
Come and behold Him, born the King of Angels;
O come, let us adore Him, O come, let us adore Him,
O come, let us adore Him, Christ the Lord.

Sing, choirs of angels, sing in exultation,
Sing, all ye citizens of heaven above:
"Glory to God in the highest";
O come, let us adore Him, O come, let us adore Him,
O come, let us adore Him, Christ the Lord.

THE CHRISTMAS STORY

TOLD BY GERTRUDE CRAMPTON

LONG, long ago, the armies of Rome conquered all the world. The head of the armies, Caesar Augustus, decided to have all the conquered people counted, each one in his own home town.

One of the people who had to make a long trip home was Joseph, a carpenter from Nazareth. Joseph and his wife, Mary, had to travel all the way to Bethlehem.

When Mary and Joseph got to Bethlehem, they were very tired. But there was not a room to be had in the town.

At last, an hotel keeper said that Mary and Joseph could sleep in his stable. There were many animals in the stable, but Mary and Joseph did not mind them.

While they were in Bethlehem, Mary had a baby. And how happy Mary and Joseph were! Everybody loves a baby. But Mary was especially happy because an angel had told her that her baby was God's son. Mary knew that her baby would help people love one another, and love God.

Of course, there was no crib in the stable. So Mary wrapped the baby and put him in a manger.

In the fields outside Bethlehem there were shepherds who watched over great flocks of sheep. Soon after Baby Jesus was born, an angel of the Lord came down to these shepherds and said to them, "Do not be afraid, I bring you good news. In Bethlehem was born a Savior, Christ the Lord. You will find the baby lying in a manger."

And many angels came, and the air was filled with their singing as they praised God and said, "Glory to God in the highest and peace on earth to men of good will."

After the angels had gone, the shepherds decided to go to Bethlehem and find the baby. One shepherd stayed to watch over all the flocks, and the others set off.

They hurried to Bethlehem, and just as the angel had told them, they found Mary and Joseph, and the babe lying in a manger.

When the shepherds left the stable, they praised God and told everyone about the angels. But before they went, they told Mary and Joseph.

And I am sure they knelt down to worship the Christ Child, and to smile at Him with all their love.

WE THREE KINGS OF ORIENT ARE

By John H. Hopkins, Jr.

We three kings of O - ri - ent are, Bear - ing gifts we tra - verse far.

Field and foun - tain, moor and moun - tain Fol - low - ing yon - der star.

Chorus

Oh,— star of won - der, star of might, Star with roy - al beau - ty bright,

West - ward lead - ing, still pro - ceed - ing, Guide us to the per - fect light.

THE NIGHT BEFORE CHRISTMAS

BY CLEMENT C. MOORE

Twas the night before Christmas when all through the house
Not a creature was stirring, not even a mouse;
The stockings were hung by the chimney with care,
In hopes that Saint Nicholas soon would be there;
The children were nestled all snug in their beds
While visions of sugar-plums danced in their heads;
And mama in her kerchief, and I in my cap,
Had just settled our brains for a long winter's nap—
When out on the lawn there arose such a clatter,
I sprang from my bed to see what was the matter.
Away to the window I flew like a flash,
Tore open the shutters and threw up the sash.
The moon on the breast of the new-fallen snow
Gave a lustre of midday to objects below;
When what to my wondering eyes should appear,
But a miniature sleigh and eight tiny reindeer,
With a little old driver, so lively and quick
I knew in a moment it must be Saint Nick!

More rapid than eagles his coursers they came,
  And he whistled and shouted
and called them by name:
"Now, Dasher! now, Dancer! now, Prancer and Vixen!
On, Comet! on, Cupid! on, Donder and Blitzen!
To the top of the porch, to the top of the wall!
Now dash away, dash away, dash away all!"
As dry leaves that before the wild hurricane fly,
When they meet with an obstacle, mount to the sky,
So up to the house-top the coursers they flew,
With a sleigh full of toys—and Saint Nicholas, too.
And then in a twinkling I heard on the roof
The prancing and pawing of each little hoof.
As I drew in my head, and was turning around,
Down the chimney Saint Nicholas came with a bound.
He was dressed all in fur from his head to his foot,
And his clothes were all tarnished with ashes and soot.
A bundle of toys he had flung on his back,
And he looked like a peddler just opening his pack.

His eyes, how they twinkled! his dimples, how merry!
His cheeks were like roses, his nose like a cherry;
His droll little mouth was drawn up like a bow,
And the beard on his chin was as white as the snow.
The stump of a pipe he held tight in his teeth,
And the smoke it encircled his head like a wreath.
He had a broad face and a little round belly
That shook, when he laughed, like a bowl full of jelly.
He was chubby and plump—a right jolly old elf;
And I laughed when I saw him, in spite of myself.
A wink of his eye and a twist of his head
Soon gave me to know I had nothing to dread.

He spoke not a word, but went straight to his work,
And filled all the stockings; then turned with a jerk,
And laying his finger aside of his nose,
And giving a nod, up the chimney he rose.
He sprang in his sleigh, to his team gave a whistle,
And away they all flew like the down of a thistle;
But I heard him exclaim, ere he drove out of sight:
"Happy Christmas to all, to all a good night!"

O LITTLE TOWN OF BETHLEHEM

By Phillips Brooks

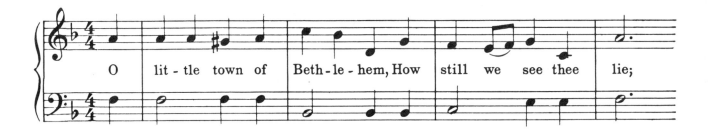

O lit - tle town of Beth - le - hem, How still we see thee lie;

A - bove thy deep and dream-less sleep The si - lent stars go by.

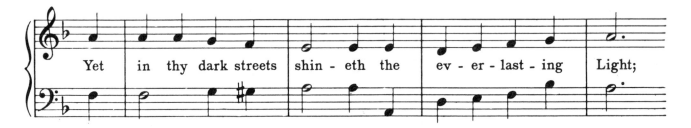

Yet in thy dark streets shin - eth the ev - er - last - ing Light;

The hopes and fears of all the years Are met in thee to - night.